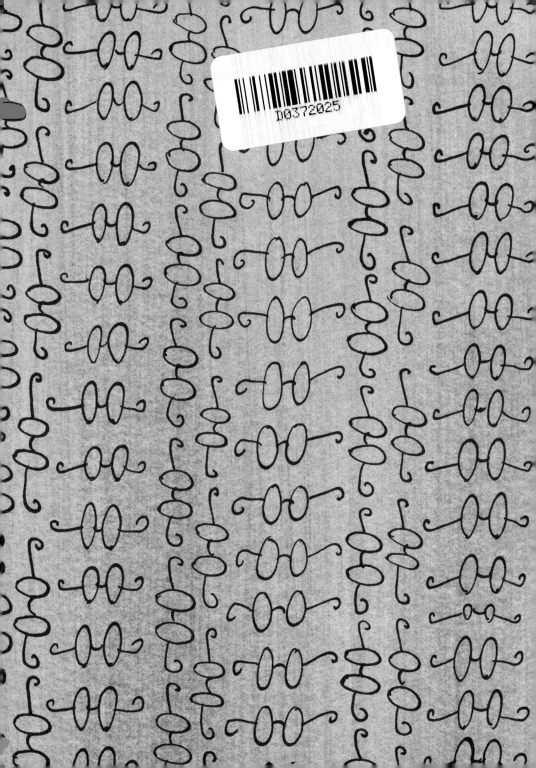

For my quartet of nephews—
Fauske, Jiks, Tim and Torre—
and for Lena—JA

For Margriet—SP

This is an Em Querido book
Published by Levine Querido

LEVINE QUERIDO

www.levinequerido.com · info@levinequerido.com

Levine Querido is distributed by Chronicle Books LLC

Text copyright © 2019 by Joukje Akveld
Illustrations copyright © 2012 by Sieb Posthuma
Translation copyright © 2021 by Bill Nagelkerke

Originally published in the Netherlands by Querido

Library of Congress Control Number: 2020937513
ISBN 978-1-64614-039-8

Printed and bound in China

MIX
Paper from
responsible sources
FSC
www.fsc.org FSC™ C104723

Published in April 2021
First Printing

Book design by Patrick Collins
The text type was set in Italian Old Style MT

WHAT OLLIE SAW

BY **JOUKJE AKVELD**

ILLUSTRATED BY **SIEB POSTHUMA**

TRANSLATED BY BILL NAGELKERKE

LQ

LEVINE QUERIDO

MONTCLAIR · AMSTERDAM · NEW YORK

Look, there's Ollie.

Maybe you already know him.

No?

In that case, we'll introduce him.

So, this is Ollie.

He has a father and a mother.

And a sister he sometimes wishes
he didn't have.

But this book isn't about Ollie's sister.

Not really.

It's about Ollie.

This is his story.

Ollie's sister—

(*So it's about his sister after all?*

Be patient. It's nearly Ollie's turn.)

Ollie's sister was bigger.

And older.

So far, so good.

Except, she grizzled a lot.

And she always thought she knew best.

Ollie kept quiet then.

Ollie and his family often went out and about.

On excursions. Visiting.

Little trips, here and there.

"Happy Family Time," Ollie's mom called it.
"Sharing adventures," Ollie's dad added.
Ollie's sister usually grizzled: "If only I could
have an ice cream."
Ollie wouldn't have minded, just once in a while,
adventuring by himself.
Without his sister.
Without grizzling.
Without sisterly-grizzles.
But his mom might not have thought it was
Happy Family Time if he said that.
So Ollie kept quiet.
And looked for a spot by the window.

As the train went through the countryside,
Ollie's sister began to yawn.

"Cows," she said. "How dull."

Then Ollie looked at his sister.

His sister who always knew better.

Ollie couldn't understand how a sister like that could be so wrong.

Cows? he thought.

COWS?!

Those were water buffalo.

Snorting water buffalo with sharp horns.

And hooves…

(Ollie chuckled to himself)

...hooves that could squash any sister,
no matter how big she was.

When they visited grandma, Ollie's mom
would take the car.
Grandma lived in a village.
No train stopped there.
Not even a bus.
They usually went on a day
when other people were driving.
The nose-to-tail traffic moved so slowly.
And Ollie's sister began to grizzle.

"Cars," she said, "are such a dumb idea."

Ollie looked at his sister.

His sister who always knew better.

He shook his head in disbelief.

You might be older, he thought. And bigger.

But you don't see clearly.

Of course they weren't just ordinary cars.

OF COURSE NOT.

They were part of a parade. A circus parade.

With acrobats in red jackets...

…and a sea lion that was able to do more
with its nose than his sister ever could,
even if she tried.

On Sundays they went sailing.

Then Ollie's father stood at the helm.

"*Oink-snortle-grunt*," his father sang.

"Fair wind, fair weather."

The waves splashed.

The sun shimmered.

But Ollie's sister began to sigh.

"So boring," she said. "Such a slowpoke boat."

Ollie looked at his sister.

His sister who always knew better.

Actually, thought Ollie, I've got a very
silly sister.

A slowpoke boat.

A SLOWPOKE BOAT?!

Oink-snortle-grunt.

A pirate ship, that's what it was.

With super-savvy pirates…

...who knew exactly what to do
with silly sisters.

Silly sister, thought Ollie.

Silly sister who doesn't see clearly.

Silly sister who doesn't see clearly and who
gets everything wrong.

"YOU'RE the one who doesn't see right, Ollie.
You need glasses!" Ollie's sister would say.

Well, there was one thing Ollie knew
for SURE: he didn't need glasses.

But Ollie's teacher thought differently.

She had a pointer.
She had a bow.
She had a very determined look.

And she thought she was always right.
(She looked a bit like Ollie's sister.)

Ollie sat in the front row.

Next to Bea. Who sat beside Gus.

Gus, Bea, Ollie.

Their teacher pointed with the pointer.

Perhaps she'll call on Gus, thought Ollie.

Perhaps Bea.

But their teacher did not call on Gus.

Or Bea.

She called on Ollie.

Ollie stood up.

He went to the board.

"Hold on," said the teacher. "Not so close."

Ollie stopped.

He tilted his head.

Left.

Right.

And left again.

"Well?" said the teacher.

She tapped with her pointer.

Ollie said: "Bird with a big pointy beak, and then a whole lot more."

Someone laughed.

(That someone was Gus.)

Someone else laughed.

(That someone else was Bea.)

And someone sighed.

(That someone was the teacher. Her ears quivered from it.)

The teacher pointed again.

Ollie took a step forward.

"No, no," said the teacher.

Ollie stopped.

He tilted his head.

Right.

Left.

And right again.

"Well?" said the teacher.

She tapped with her pointer.

Ollie said: "Fish with tails,
in the deep sea."

More laughter.
(From Gus.)
(And also from Bea.)
But no sigh.

The teacher put her pointer in a corner
and said: "Ollie, you need glasses."

Ollie didn't think so.

OF COURSE NOT.

But his mother did.

And so did his father.

And so did Ollie's sister. Especially her.

("I *knew* it," she said.)

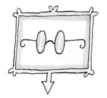

It was four against one.

You'll know who didn't get his way...

...and where Ollie had to go.

"Better?" asked Ollie's mother.

"Better?" asked Ollie's father.

"Better?" asked Ollie's sister and his teacher.

Ollie said nothing.

His thoughts went back.
Back to the cows and the cars.
Back to the boat, and the board
in his classroom.

"Well," said Ollie.

He frowned.

He scratched.

He pondered.

(Until his face was positively puckered.)

"WELL?!"
asked Ollie's mother,
Ollie's father,
Ollie's sister,
and his teacher.

They held their breath.

"Well, no."

Because Ollie was sure, very, very sure,
that he didn't need glasses...

...at least, not all of the time.

SOME NOTES
ON THIS BOOK'S PRODUCTION

Sieb Posthuma began his creation of the artwork for this book
with much pig-sketching practice to make sure he rendered
Ollie exactly right. When Sieb was ready to move to final art,
he began by using Ecoline (liquid watercolor paint) on paper for
the background, and then drew lines over it with pencil.
He made the lines final with East Indian ink (black ink),
and then erased pencil lines that were still visible. For final
coloring, he used further Ecoline. Sieb paid particular attention
to the endpapers, which portray almost 500 pairs of glasses.

The text was set in Italian Old Style MT,
created by a staff designer at Monotype in 1911.
It was influenced by ITC Golden Type, which was designed by
William Morris, Sigrid Engelmann,
and Helga Jörgenson in 1890.

The case for the book was printed on 128gsm Oji Zunma FSC
glossy art paper with matte laminate, and features touches
of spot UV. The book's interior was printed on 120gsm
UPM FSC-certified woodfree paper and bound in China.

Production was supervised by Leslie Cohen and Freesia Blizard
Book cover and interiors designed by Patrick Collins
Edited by Arthur A. Levine

LQ
LEVINE QUERIDO

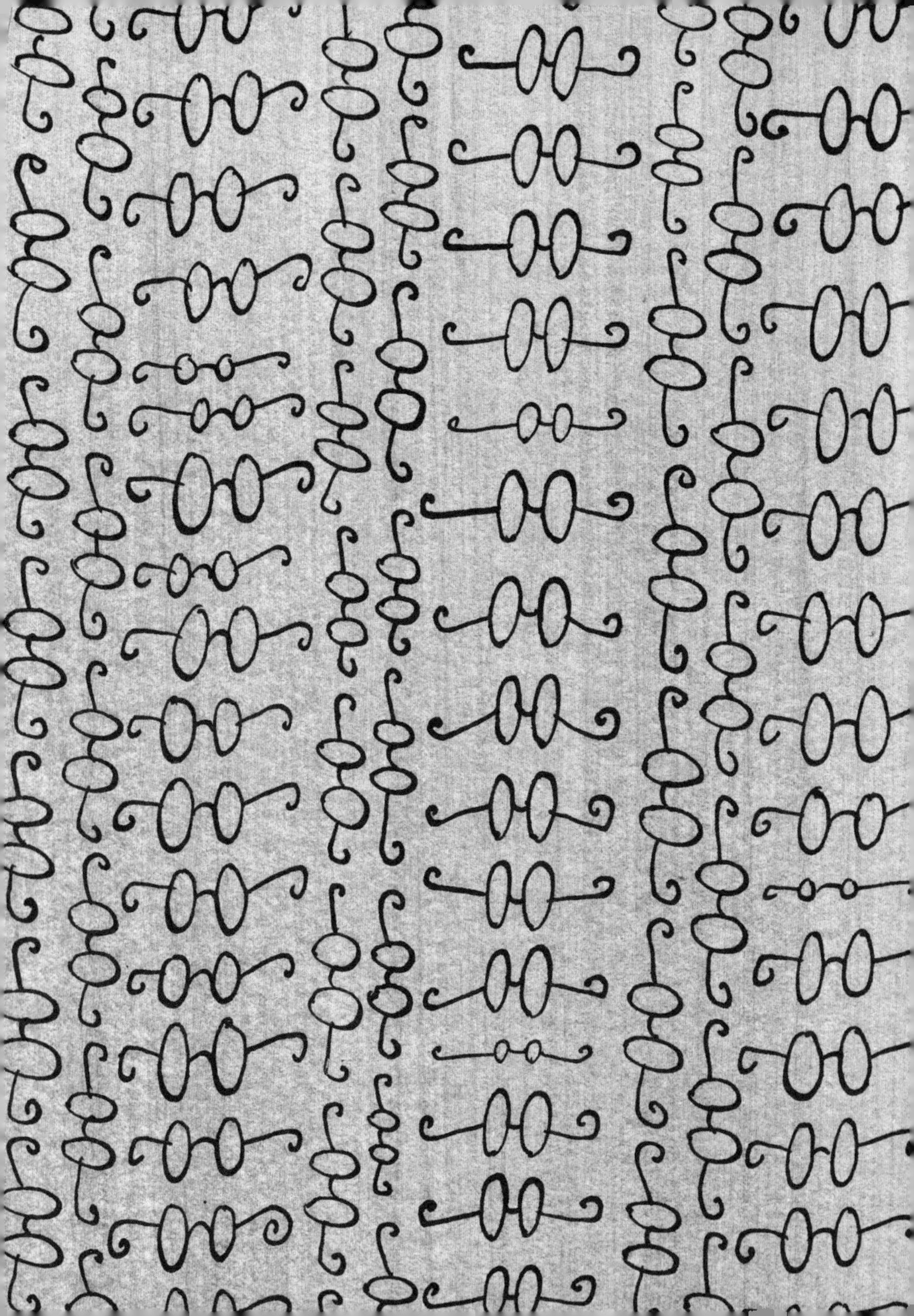